The 10 Best Things About My Dad

By Christine Loomis

Illustrated by Jackie Urbanovic

SCHOLASTIC INC. Cartwheel B·O·O·K·S®

New York   Toronto   London   Auckland   Sydney
Mexico City   New Delhi   Hong Kong   Buenos Aires

For great dads everywhere
— C.L.

For my dad, who taught me to love
working with my hands.
— J.U.

ISBN 0-439-57769-1

Text copyright © 2004 by Christine Loomis.
Illustrations copyright © 2004 by Jackie Urbanovic.
All rights reserved. Published by Scholastic Inc.
SCHOLASTIC, CARTWHEEL BOOKS, and associated logos
are trademarks and/or registered trademarks of Scholastic Inc.

Library of Congress Cataloging-in-Publication Data

Loomis, Christine.
 The 10 best things about my dad / by Christine Loomis ; illustrated by Jackie Urbanovic.
   p.   cm.
   Summary: A child describes his father, who is loving, supportive, caring, and fun.
   ISBN 0-439-57769-1 (pbk.)
   [1. Father and child — Fiction. 2. Stories in rhyme.] I. Title: Ten best things about my dad. II. Urbanovic, Jackie, ill. III. Title.
   PZ8.3.L8619Aae 2004
 [E] — dc21   2003009780

20 19 18 17 16 15 14   09 10 11 12
           Printed in the U.S.A. • First printing, May 2004

Do you know what the ten best things are about my dad? I'll tell you!

He can throw,

he can bat,

he likes hoops and balls and gloves.

But playing *anything* with me
is what Dad really loves.

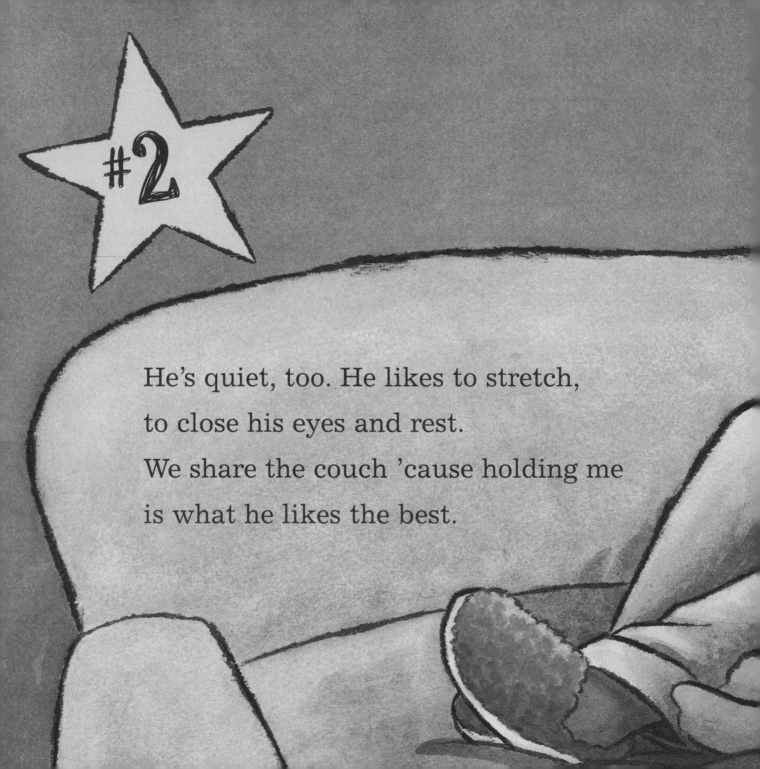

He's quiet, too. He likes to stretch,
to close his eyes and rest.
We share the couch 'cause holding me
is what he likes the best.

He teaches me the stuff he's learned,
like knowing right from wrong.

If I mess up he says, "No sweat,
you'll get it before long."

When I perform he's always there,
cheering right out loud.

He cheers the same if I'm the star
or just part of the crowd.

We go for drives because it's fun
to ride around and roam.

Sometimes I think we're lost—but then he always gets us home.

He reads me bedtime stories,
sometimes nine or ten.

He NEVER argues when I say,
"Please read that one AGAIN!"

He understands if I'm afraid

even late at night.

He knows how to scare monsters
until THEY leave in fright.

When I'm sad he hugs me close.

He never says, "Don't cry."

He's very good at listening.

He's just that kind of guy.

Sometimes he's so silly.

He's good at tickling, too!

He tells bad jokes and makes me laugh
when I am feeling blue.

But here's what is the best of all,
better than one through nine.
My dad is extra special—

just because he's mine!